The Straggler Defenders

A True Story of Dispersion of Afghan National Army Soldiers

By Zahra Mushtaq

Translated by

Asadullah Jafari "Pezhman"

Ukiyoto Publishing

All global publishing rights are held by

Ukiyoto Publishing

Published in 2024

Content Copyright © Zahra Mushtaq

ISBN 9789361724121

All rights reserved.

No part of this publication may be reproduced, transmitted, or stored in a retrieval system, in any form by any means, electronic, mechanical, photocopying, recording or otherwise, without the prior permission of the publisher.

The moral rights of the author have been asserted.

This book is sold subject to the condition that it shall not by way of trade or otherwise, be lent, resold, hired out or otherwise circulated, without the publisher's prior consent, in any form of binding or cover other than that in which it is published.

www.ukiyoto.com

Preface

In the somber aftermath of Afghanistan's fall to the Taliban, the echoes of despair reverberate across the borders of this country, transcending nationalities and binding fates. *"The Straggler Defenders"* is a compelling work of non-fiction penned by the Iranian journalist Ms. Zahra Mushtaq. This true story unravels the harrowing and displacement narrative of the Afghanistan National Army soldiers who sought refuge in Iran; their escape etched against the backdrop of a nation that has plunged into chaos. As the dust settled on the war-torn landscapes of Afghanistan, a tide of displacement swept through the courageous men who once stood as defenders of their homeland named Afghanistan. Zahra Mushtaq, known for her keen observations and compassionate storytelling, delves into the untold stories of these Straggler Defenders—soldiers who sought shelter and refuge across the Iranian borders in the face of adversity, injustice, and disloyalty.

As the characters navigate the challenges of seeking refuge in Iran, Ms. Mushtaq skillfully weaves a tapestry of human and soldier experiences, exploring the intricate web of emotions accompanying the quest for safety amidst the chaos of war and collapse in Afghanistan. "The Straggler Defenders" stands as a testament to the indomitable human spirit, the bonds formed in adversity, and the pursuit of hope and safety when confronted with the shadows of displacement, betrayal, and brutality by corrupt Afghan politicians. So, through the lens of Ms. Zahra Mushtaq's narrative, readers embark on a poignant journey—one that illuminates the untold facets of escape, resilience, and the search for a semblance of homeland when the familiars, house, and homeland crumbles away.

Cordially
Asadullah Jafari "Pezhman"

March 4, 2024

On August 15, 2021, following the fall of Kabul City to the hands of the Taliban group and the districts of Afghanistan, a wave of ordinary refugees and nearly 3,000 Afghan national army soldiers in various ranks, from high-ranking army officers to regular soldiers, fled to the borders of Iran. These soldiers, some of whom were on foot and more of them with special vehicles and military equipment. After surrendering their weapons, they were resettled in several border camps inside the territory of Iran. Their settlement in the provinces of Sistan and Baluchistan in the south-east of Iran, whose people always face severe livelihood problems, especially water shortages and numerous deaths of people infected with the coronavirus, imposed a double burden. Although local benefactors came to help the soldiers in the first days, gradually and with the prolongation of these army soldiers' stay, serious thought had to be given to food, clothing, and other necessary things.

Contents

A Bitter Narrative of a Camp on the Border Between Iran and Afghanistan   1

Return to Afghanistan   2

Fear and Desperation Were Flashing in their Eyes   4

The Taliban Infiltrators   5

Why Didn't You Fight for Your Country?   7

The Free Water Has Run Out   9

The Answers Are Sad   11

It's not Really a Nice Fate   13

The Straggler Defenders   14

General Amnesty   16

Human Traffickers and Afghan Refugees   17

A Hot Summery Day   20

About the Author   *21*

About the Translator   *22*

A Bitter Narrative of a Camp on the Border Between Iran and Afghanistan

Shahin Ghorzahi, known as Arbabi, and I, who are among Iranian philanthropists and active social activists, especially in Sistan and Baluchistan province in the south-east of Iran, departure and went to the border between the two countries to help the Afghan army soldiers. The first step of our work was to buy several three-thousand-liter water sources, install and fill them with clean water, and buy daily ice for the displaced and straggler soldiers.

Of course, I had also announced a call for help in the "Gurohey Nikookaran-e Iranzamin" (Philanthropists of Iran Land Group) to provide the necessary funds to buy daily food for these displaced and straggler soldiers. The efforts that started on August 16 continued until the end of August. Meanwhile, besides the serious support of several other charities, it is impossible not to mention the empathy and responsibility of the Islamic Republic of Iran Army in helping Afghan military refugees. In those days, I often witnessed the hospitality of Iranian army officers who kindly shared their food rations with the refugees and homeless Afghan soldiers. But their story was a bitter one.

Return to Afghanistan

It is worth considering that both groups had their own problems. It seemed impossible to apply for asylum for those soldiers who wanted to join their families as well, considering all the current difficulties in Iran. On the other hand, except for the few described in the report, the other soldiers in the camp did not want to return to Afghanistan. Because returning to Afghanistan meant being shot dead by the Taliban fighters. However, after the arrival of the United Nations High Commissioner for Refugees staff (UNHCR) and the assurance letter announced by the Taliban group that they would not harm the displaced soldiers, all the camps were evacuated, and the soldiers were returned to Afghanistan against their will by land route. Therefore, the international community is expected to oblige and bind the Taliban to save the lives of these three thousand army soldiers by using its executive organs.

During this period, many messages were received from Afghans who were grateful for the support of the military forces who took refuge in Iran. However, some others wanted to know in the most substantial possible tone why they had surrendered the country to the Taliban so easily. So, I participated in several Instagram Live shows and tried to be an honest witness to what I saw. But the most important was attending a live meeting using Zoom. In this meeting, which was held on August 29, 2021, many prominent Australian civil activists and representatives of the country's parliament were present. As a journalist and social activist, I had a five-minute speaking opportunity. I participated in this conference because by joining with other human rights activists, I could help increase the acceptance of Afghan military refugees. That's why I tried to convey my greatest wish to them in the shortest possible words: "I believe that the future world will be in the hands of responsible people who help and respect each other regardless of borders, religion, and beliefs."

Fear and Desperation Were Flashing in their Eyes

I was standing very close face to face with the soldiers and young officers of a shattered army who had fled from the Taliban group. I conducted field interviews with displaced people that day, and they spoke of the pain of statelessness and dispersion. Many of them had fear, worry, and desperation in their eyes. While wearing thick military uniforms and boots, they spent long days in the border immigration camp under harsh conditions. They only wanted one thing: Granting asylum to themselves and their families who were in danger of death in Afghanistan.

The Taliban Infiltrators

I was sure that my country, Iran, would not be able to accept them for many reasons. Their number was nearly 3,000 officers and soldiers. Among them, only a few wanted to return to Afghanistan. Their colleagues introduced people who were willing to return easily as Taliban infiltrators. But others seriously wanted to stay and said that if Iran did not accept us, they would send us to another Muslim country. But all of them were taken back to Afghanistan against their will one morning by the buses in front of the camp.

The day before, representatives of the United Nations High Commissioner for Refugees staff (UNHCR), and apparently with the mediation of Taliban envoys, met with these soldiers and gave them a letter of protection. However, the next day, these soldiers were returned to Afghanistan along with their war equipment and weapons. The Taliban infiltrators are nothing new, and they were the ones who were themselves members of the Afghan National Army and always sent their peers to death.

Since then, I don't know if the soldiers I interviewed that day are still alive. But the deep common sufferings we shared in those few days are so bitter that I shall never forget them. The world's people should be from the Middle East to understand what we are talking about when discussing suffering and pain. Big and Immigrant-receiving states are obliged to share a part of their happiness, prosperity, and peace with the people of Afghanistan and all the oppressed people of the Middle East by increasing the capacity to accept more vulnerable refugees.

Why Didn't You Fight for Your Country?

I don't know if that small stature army officer who stood face to face with me in the "Shahid Madani Camp" is still alive or not! I won't write his name here not to kill or cause him more harm. He was the voice of 3000 military soldiers, requesting asylum-seeking for all of them in Iran. I was not angry, but with a highly trembling voice and a painful lump in his throat, I asked him and everyone with whom I had the opportunity to speak, why did you not fight for your country? Why did you run away, and why did you let your country fall city by city and fall into the hands of the Taliban group? I gave them the example of Iran's eight-year war, where "we, men and women, fought against the enemy."

I was trying hard to hide my trembling voice and crying eyes under the hat I had pulled down to my eyebrows and the mask that covered my entire face. It was Wednesday, August 16, 2021. A man brought himself close to my face and said in a firm tone that if we had fought, hundreds of civilians would have been killed because the Taliban had hidden themselves in the houses of ordinary people. However, we did not fight so that no one would be killed. My voice got louder. With all those weapons? You should not have given up. Something in me wants to scream and not believe anything. The man answered that we had weapons. They had too much. If we had ten guns, they had a hundred. If we had one tank, they had ten. The Taliban were strong.

The soldiers had come a long way. They had reached the border on foot and riding the latest American model tanks. They had entered Iran's Sistan and Baluchistan province from the Milk border crossing with all their weapons and nearly a hundred vehicles. There were so many of them! Too many! Three thousand people! The Kabul city had not fallen yet. However, the easy and meaningful surrender of the cities showed that the capital would also fail. That day, all the world's essential and even ordinary news networks were talking about an unexpected incident in Afghanistan.

The Free Water Has Run Out

The soldiers had fled to Iran with all the ammunition they had with them. Three thousand soldiers were accommodated in various camps, including Shahid Madani School in the village of Karga Pakak in Nimroz district and Mulla Sharif checkpoint in Zahak city. In the first days, some high-ranking officers were sent to Kabul by plane, but as soon as the city of Kabul fell, it was no longer possible to send the rest of the military. Even hearing the name of the Taliban frightens everyone. In the hot air of Sistan-Baluchistan, the soldiers were lying in the courtyard and school rooms with thick overalls. Everyone was sitting somewhere. Soldiers were sitting there on the toilet walls. An ordinary school near the Hirmand district lacked the capacity and conditions to become a camp for three hundred people.

The mats spread out in the classrooms and the hallways, which looked worn and archaic, once belonged to the rural students of this boarding school. There was no bathroom; the soldiers poured water on their heads and bodies with a hose in the schoolyard or inside the toilets. They had not taken off their thick clothes for days and had nothing else to wear except military boots. They have entered a province that is one of the most water-poor or the most dehydrated provinces in the country, and a part of this region is located just a few kilometers from the Kamal Khan Dam on the big Hirmand River. The same dam that, on its opening day, Ashraf Ghani, the fugitive president of Afghanistan, proudly said, "Free water has run out. From now on, water will be exchanged for oil." On that day, Ashraf Ghani did not know that he and his country would soon fall into the hands of the Taliban group and that his country's soldiers would ask for asylum from Iran in a sad circumstance.

There were two groups of soldiers in Shahid Madani's school: those who wanted to stay and those who wanted to leave. About 63 out of 300 people had carefree and indifferent faces. Those who tried to go said the Taliban had nothing to do with them. But other soldiers secretly told me they were Taliban infiltration forces among the insiders. After a few days, they returned the soldiers' mobile phones to themselves. Some had witnessed their contact with the Taliban forces, and these suspicious contacts made the soldiers more and more afraid because they had given the Taliban the statistics of military personnel and equipment that they had delivered to the Iranian army and border forces. In front of me were many desperate faces anxiously requesting asylum from Iran, which has housed the most prominent Afghan refugees for many years. Iran seemed unlikely to want or be able to add other immigrants to its list in the current situation.

The Answers Are Sad

I wondered and questioned how they managed to leave their families and run away. But the answers are sad. They were soldiers who had not seen their families, wives, and children for many months, even more than a year; this is because their service and military positions were far away from where their families lived, and they often did not have the financial means to go to their cities and visit their families. Their great art was to have military jobs and send money to their wives and children.

One of the soldiers told me about his little children: Mujib and Azadeh! He did not know if the wife and children were still alive or not after the attack by the Taliban group! He didn't know if he would see them again or not! But other soldiers insisted on seeking asylum. They wanted their families to come to Iran and become Iranian citizens. Their dream seemed so far away that I was afraid to imagine it. They were talking about the possibility of being shot by the Taliban if they returned to Afghanistan, and their most immense suffering was the families with many children whom these soldiers were only breadwinners for them. They said the new government and regime will cancel our salaries, and our children will starve. Even if the Taliban do not hunt them from house to house because of our jobs, they will die of hunger and poverty.

I was afraid of the eyes of some of them. There was frightening violence in the eyes of some of them, and I did not know what would have happened between us if they and I had not been in the current location. Were those who looked at me with a specific look, with looks of indifference and fear, really the infiltrators of the Taliban among the Afghan army who had taken refuge in Iran?

It's not Really a Nice Fate

Shahid Madani School was more like a defeated battlefield than a school, with no hopeful signs except for deep suffering on those hot summer days. In that hot pyramid, I saw the school's principal, whose mouth opened and closed due to the heat of the air, and he talked about the damage caused in his school. Sometimes he was furious; broken glasses and a burnt electric water cooler that did not have enough power to give cold water to three hundred thirsty, tired, and hungry soldiers. Soldiers who wore the same thick military uniforms for long days smelled of sweat and had no clothes to change. Maybe even their toes were crushed and rotten inside the boots. The janitor of the school was talking about his family being imprisoned:

"The janitor's family has not left the janitory's house for about two weeks. Where do they come? How to cross the yard full of soldiers and where to go? The janitor's father-in-law, who recently had an eye surgery, was also stuck in this crowd. If he left there, there would be no one to take care of him. Afghan National Army soldiers are sitting or walking in the yard. It is not really a beautiful fate to not know what will happen to you tomorrow. Either you will be alive or you will be executed! You will become a refugee or you will be handed over to your enemy, the Taliban!"

The Straggler Defenders

It's just one day later. One day, after distributing several hot meals to the displaced soldiers and defenders! Three hundred Balochi clothes, toothbrushes, toothpaste, newly bought slippers, and men who are now familiar to you, their smell, their particular look, and their pains, which were told to me by their representative. Similar stories and their shared human sufferings are bitter and unforgettable. One of the army soldiers extended his hand to me. He had some old and tattered Afghani cash in his fist. He begged me to buy Nas or Naswar for him from the shop. I know what Nas is. [Nās or Naswār or maybe "Snuff" is the name of an addictive herbal drug which is made from tobacco leaves; Nas is green in color and has a pungent taste and smell; this substance is mostly made in Afghanistan regions]. Many people in Iran's Sistan and Baluchistan province also use Nas.

Naswar is a type of drug that many young people are addicted to nowadays; young people who just open their eyes start to use Naswar. However, passengers and shops have ten types of Naswar for sale on their shelves and pockets. I laughed and told the soldier it was better to stop using Nas as much as possible. Nevertheless, some villager children were looking at the soldiers of the Afghan National Army from behind closed bars, insulting and cursing them. They were calling them "Cowards, Traitors, and Deserters." My eyes are tied to the eyes of Mujib and Azadeh's father, and tears flow from both of our eyes; this was not something simple. It was the issue that the national defenders of a developing country were displaced. Each of them had stories, and their stories are bitter narratives that I called the story of these soldiers "Straggler or Displaced Defenders," defenders who no longer have a homeland.

General Amnesty

Now is the day after yesterday. United Nations High Commissioner for Refugees staff (UNHCR) have come to Edimi camp. Now, all camp officials have become stricter and more serious. No one pays attention to us. They won't let us into the camp. The camp is located in the Department of Foreign Nationals and Immigrants Affairs. The camp officials counted the soldiers and listened to their words, just like the first day they recorded their arrival time. They fingerprinted the soldiers, sent them to their bases in Afghanistan, and handed over their military equipment. UN staff tell Afghan soldiers that the Taliban has announced a "General Amnesty" they say that the Taliban has even forgiven the Afghan security forces. Although they were military, they surrendered to Iran's border forces with their military equipment and vehicles. It's now noon local time. The hot wind of Sistan and Balochistan blows strongly. It is one of those monsoon winds called the "120-day winds" of Sistan and Baluchistan.

Human Traffickers and Afghan Refugees

It is not people but the morning winds of Sistan and Baluchistan that shake the tents of the Molla Sharif camp. All the tents set up by the Red Crescent Committee for Afghan refugees are empty because the strong wind tore apart the tents. Immigrant families rejected by the police from inside Iran because they do not have an ID card do not stay in these tents for more than a day and are deported to Afghanistan. Meanwhile, a few days ago, one of the Afghan migrant women gave birth to her baby girl in these tents. Like another family who lost their nine-year-old son to death on this route, there was a family with a little girl and a nine-year-old boy.

The human traffickers brought this family from Nimroz province of Afghanistan to the Iranian border. This family has walked for a long time with fatigue and hunger. When they reached Iran's high border wall, which is several meters high, this family climbed the wall with other travelers. The wall is both long and almost 3.5 meters high. The number of Afghan refugees was extensive, including women, men, and also small children of all ages. This boundary wall is flat, black, and cement. But the women alone could not climb the wall, and then they climbed the wall with their hands by grabbing the hooked hands of the men. At that time, it is dark at night. The code sign of the night between passengers and human traffickers is green and orange laser lights; the sign of passengers on this side of the border is a green light, and the sign of passengers on the other side is orange.

At the same time, the woman and the little girl of this Afghan family climbed the wall first. After that, the man asked the family to send his son over the wall, but the human trafficker team leader said, "Go over the wall yourself first! Then I'll raise your son." When the Afghan man crossed the border wall into Iran at night, the human trafficker team leader did not pick up his son anymore. Wife and husband, with their little girl, waited behind the border wall for their son to come. The night is lit! All the passengers have fled to the plains and deserts because of fear of the border police. But still, there is no news about that child. The husband and wife only cried for their child from night to morning.

They have visited all the long border walls, crying and screaming a hundred times. The child's parents thought that their child might have been thrown to this side of the border wall from somewhere else. But it didn't happen like that either. However, out of sympathy, the border forces have visited and searched all the lines of the wall step by step with this family. Eventually, this family found their nine-year-old son on the other side of the border wall with the help of border forces police. Human traffickers had sexually assaulted the oppressed child, whose whole body was covered in blood due to consecutive and repeated assaults. The nine-year-old boy looked dead in torn to pieces clothes with his guts spilled out. But at that time, someone noticed the child's weak pulse, and they took him to the hospital very soon.

A Hot Summery Day

Many children, girls, and young women are raped and assaulted sexually by thieves and human traffickers on the way to reach the border lines between Iran and Afghanistan due to illegal immigration. But they do keep silent, perhaps except for silence, because they have no other choice. Maybe the victims think this is the last humiliation they must endure on this painful and tragic path. Perhaps they think passing through the border walls is entering the gates of happiness. Therefore, this is a part of the story of the suffering of Afghan refugees that I want to share with people of the world. What does anyone know more than this? It was a hot summer day. Everyone was struggling with an overwhelming heat. A sparrow inside one of the tents was pecking at a piece of bread that may have fallen on the ground from an Afghan refugee child.

About the Author

Zahra Mushtaq

Zahra Mushtaq is an Iranian Author, Journalist, Social Activist, Screenwriter, and Producer who graduated with a master's degree in rural development engineering from Tarbiat Modares University in Tehran. She has created many great works in the fields of cinema, literature, and journalism, the most important of them including The 13-episode documentary series One Day, One Woman, IRIB Channel 1 (2008), The documentary film Lost Identity (about an Iraqi museum looted during the fall of Saddam Hussein) Al-Alam News Network (2006) and The documentary film Lost Justice about the fall of Saddam Hussein. Also, her writings and articles have appeared in many newspapers, such as Shahrvand Newspaper, Shargh Daily, Zan Newspaper, and Hamshahri Newspaper. After the fall of the Afghan state in 2021, Ms. Mushtaq also traveled to Afghanistan, where she conducted the first interview with Taliban spokesman Zabihullah Mujahid in Kabul. Therefore, her last book, "When Mujahid Smiled; Forty Days in Afghanistan," was published in Tehran in 2022.

About the Translator

Asadullah Jafari "Pezhman"

Asadullah Jafari "Pezhman" is a Translator, Columnist, and a former member of the Afghan National Army, born in 1998 and raised in Afghanistan. His translations and writings have appeared in several online and print newspapers, magazines, and publications, including SubheKabul Daily, Basilicata24, Indian Defence Review, Hindu Post, Afghan Voices, TheCommuneMag, and VOC News. He also authored "The Heart-Wrenching August" (2023) translated "The Sounds of Destiny and The Poetry Collection" (2023). His most famous works of translation are the books (Tears from Kabul, Deliverance from Kabul, and Afghanistan's Romeo and Juliet) translated from English into Persian-Dari. Thus, Asadullah was honored and deserved appreciation in the special section for the 3rd Iranian Youth Book of the Year National Award as an Immigrant Young in 2023.

www.ingramcontent.com/pod-product-compliance
Lightning Source LLC
LaVergne TN
LVHW041602070526
838199LV00046B/2096